# THE
# FAMILY
# TREE

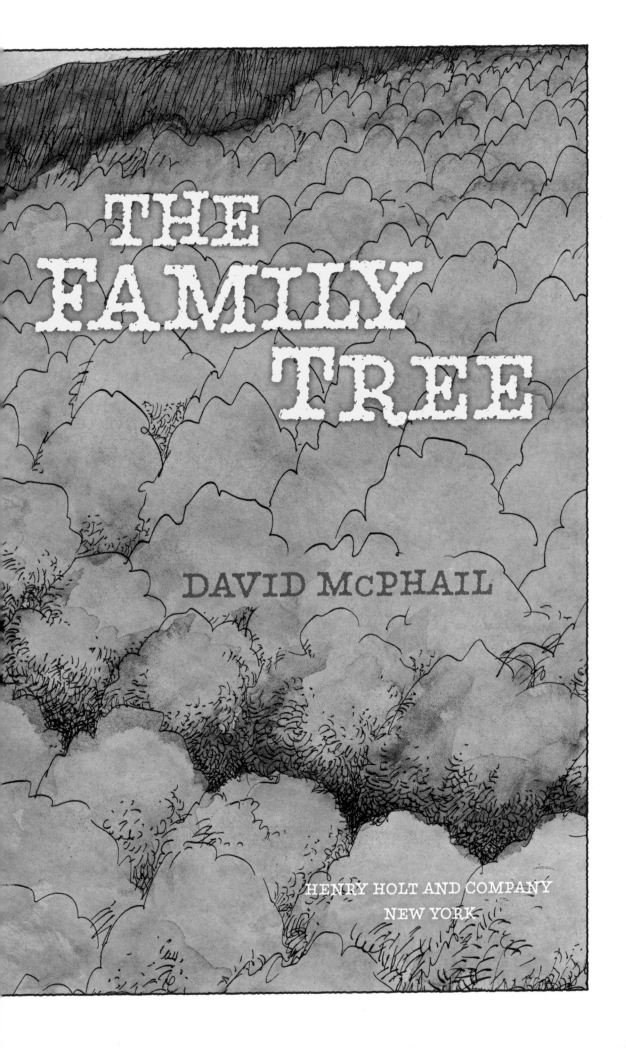

# THE FAMILY TREE

## DAVID McPHAIL

HENRY HOLT AND COMPANY
NEW YORK

Many years ago, a young man came
to the wilderness to start a new life.

He chopped down trees to make fields for his crops and pastures for his animals.

But he left one tree standing. It would provide
shade for his house during the long hot summers
and act as a buffer against the chilly winter winds.

The man used the logs to make boards
and beams for his house and barns.

He used others to make posts and rails
for his fences.

He and his oxen removed the tree stumps and dragged them to the edges of the fields.

CREEAAK

Then the man built his house.
When it was finished, he went away.

Weeks later, he returned with his wife.

Eventually, they had a child. A son.

After a while, more people came.
Now the family had neighbors.

Years passed. The man grew old.

His son took over the running of the farm,
and he had a son of his own to help him.

New generations joined the family. Old ones left.
The tree witnessed it all.

Now, the great-great-grandson of the first settler lived on the farm. The boy loved the tree. It was like a friend to him.

One day, workers came to widen the road
to make room for more cars, more trucks.

The tree was in the way—
it would have to come down.

The boy protested. He stood between the workers
and tree, and would not budge.

A call for assistance went out.

Help soon arrived.

The boy and his dog were not alone.

The workers huddled. They devised a new plan—
one that would work for everyone.

beep! bee

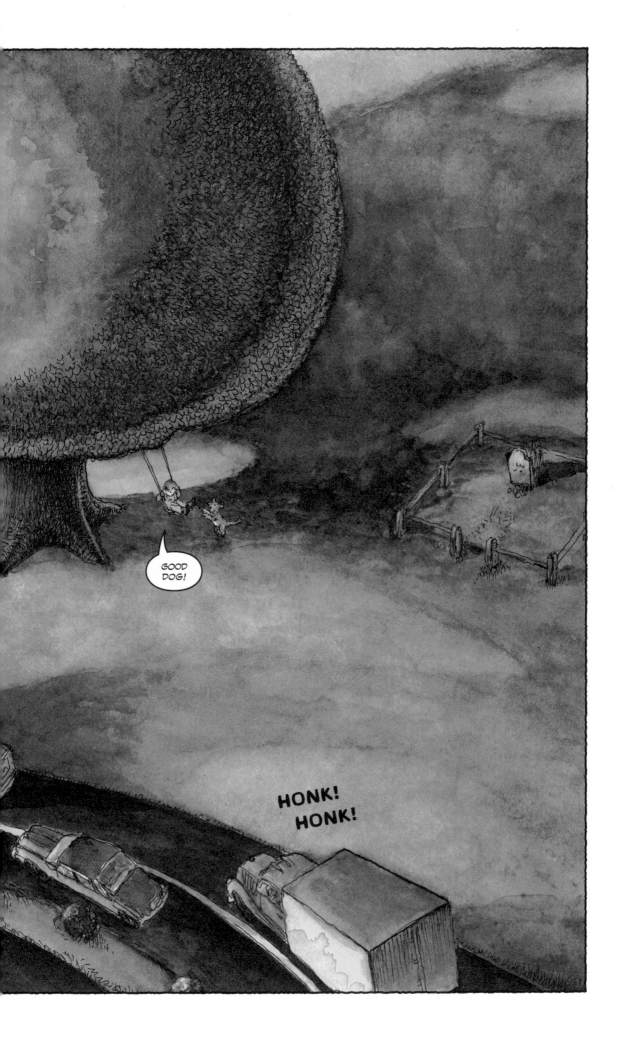

BONK!

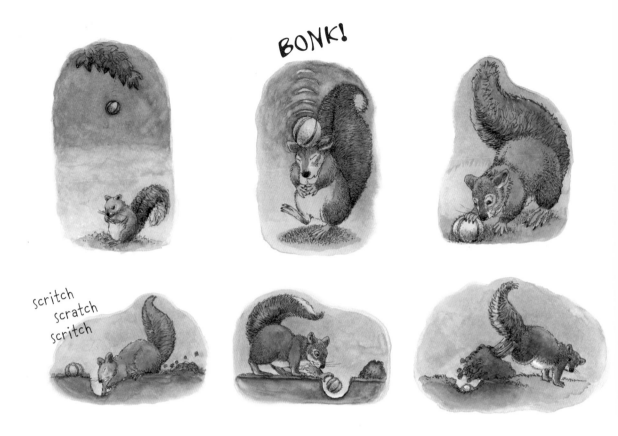

scritch
scratch
scritch

*For James—we do love trees, don't we?*

Henry Holt and Company, LLC / *Publishers since 1866*
175 Fifth Avenue, New York, New York 10010 [mackids.com]

Henry Holt® is a registered trademark of Henry Holt and Company, LLC.

Library of Congress Cataloging-in-Publication Data
McPhail, David. The family tree / David McPhail. — 1st ed.
p.    cm.
Summary: In the 1800s, a man clearing land in a beautiful forest to build a home leaves one special tree, but many years
later the tree is in trouble, and the man's great-great grandson enlists a host of animal friends to try to save it.
ISBN 978-0-8050-9057-4
[1. Trees—Fiction.  2. Environmental protection—Fiction.  3. Family life—Fiction.]  I. Title.
PZ7.M478818Fam 2011    [E]—dc22    2010011692

First Edition—2012 / Designed by Patrick Collins
The artist used watercolor and ink on illustration board to create the illustrations for this book.
Printed in December 2011 in China by Toppan Leefung Printing Ltd., Dongguan City, Guangdong Province

1  3  5  7  9  10  8  6  4  2

pitter pat
pitter pat